To Rabbittown

by APRIL HALPRIN WAYLAND
illustrated by ROBIN SPOWART

SCHOLASTIC INC.
New York Toronto London Auckland Sydney

ISBN 0-590-44777-7

Text copyright © 1989 by April Halprin Wayland.
Illustrations copyright © 1989 by Robin Spowart.
All rights reserved. Published by Scholastic Inc.
BLUE RIBBON is a registered trademark of Scholastic Inc.

12 11 10 9 8 7 6 5 4 3 2   2 3 4 5 6 7/9

Printed in the U.S.A.   24

For my mother, Saralee Halprin,
who infused me with the music of our
language, and who inspires me
with the language of her music. And
for my father, Leahn J. Halprin,
who honored all my questions, whose
imagination was limitless.

—A. H.W.

To Tom Durkin.

—R.S.

I opened her rabbit-y cage
and while she nibbled celery
I asked her:
Where do the rolling hills go?
She said:
Beyond the wheat
to a pine forest
to the edge of it all
to Rabbittown

I snuggled her close
She told me:
Hop there
Ride the green waves
Find the cliffs
past the smell of the sea
There you'll find
those brown rabbit eyes
And so I went

They sniffed me and I asked:
How long have you been here?

And what do you eat
in Rabbittown?

The wooly one spoke
She said:
Here before the moon
we drink milk from the milk grass
eat pine needle salad
and save waterlilies for dessert

They told me:
Stay
I sat with them
burrowed with them
played games with their babies
and sliced pine branches
at dusk

I grew ears
I heard butterflies fly
I heard the movement of worms in the soil
I heard clouds coming

I wrinkled my rabbit nose
I smelled the approaching storm
I smelled the difference
between brown rabbits and spotted rabbits
I smelled their soft love for me

I hopped on my new rabbit legs
Every patch of ground

tickled the pinks of my paws
tickled me into the air and across the green hills

They taught me rabbit songs
morning smell-the-air songs
lunching-on-wheat songs
rose and earthworm songs
that only rabbits sing
and only rabbits hear

With my brown rabbit eyes
I found delicious pine roots
saw rain before it splashed
watched quick rabbits stand still
when fox eyes passed by

In my fur
I was warm in the morning frost
and comfortable on the hard rocks
And the little ones leaned on me
as they slept

One snuggled close and asked:
Where do the rolling hills go?
I said:
Beyond the pine forest
to fields of wheat
to houses filled with the people I love

I said:
I miss them
I want to run back through the hills
to the tops of the cliffs

toward the smell of mown lawns
where I'll find
those curious human eyes

And off I hopped
through the pine forest
over the rolling wheat hills
past the smell of the sea
back to mown lawns
and my family

To grow legs again
to grow arms again
to hold my pet bunny again
who holds memories
of Rabbittown.